FASHIONS OF THE OLD SOUTH
Coloring Book

TOM TIERNEY

DOVER PUBLICATIONS
Garden City, New York

Bibliographical Note

Fashions of the Old South Coloring Book is a new work, first published by Dover Publications in 2004.

International Standard Book Number

ISBN-13: 978-0-486-43876-4
ISBN-10: 0-486-43876-7

Manufactured in the United States of America
43876714   2023
www.doverpublications.com

INTRODUCTION

The American Civil War, also known as the War Between the States, began with the secession of South Carolina from the United States on December 20, 1860. Soon, ten other states had followed suit, creating an eleven-state Confederacy. In April 1861, President Abraham Lincoln asked the states still loyal to the federal government to put a stop to the rebellion by the Southern states. Fort Sumter, in Charleston, South Carolina, was the setting for the first shots fired in the Civil War. The bloody conflict, which continued until 1865, amassed more American deaths than any other war in U.S. history.

There were a number of issues that caused the rebellion, notably the conflict over the practice of slavery; the consideration of the extension of slavery into new territories; and a fundamental disagreement about the supremacy of the federal government over states' rights. It was a costly war, not only in the numbers killed, but also in the toll it took on the South. The defeated region was financially ruined for many years. At the end of the war, President Lincoln was assassinated, the states that had seceded were readmitted and the Union preserved, and slavery was abolished.

Although the South provided the raw cotton for the American clothing industry, the actual fabric was created in the North's New England spinning mills. Thus, Southern fashion came to an abrupt halt soon after the act of secession. For years the wealthy Southern plantation owners had "summered" in the cooler climate of the Northern states, often in summer homes along the coast of New England. While vacationing, the Southerners would stop off in New York or Boston or Philadelphia to buy the latest styles for the entire family. There were a number of fashion houses in those cities, such as G. Brodie on Canal Street in New York, whose fine workmanship generally was copied from the latest London and Paris styles. If a family was particularly well-to-do, it would make the "grand tour" of Europe every few years and come home with the latest in high fashion. The declaration of war, followed by the Northern blockade of the Southern coastline and the capture of New Orleans (1862), cut off the South's ability to sell its cotton to any other nation, thus forcing her to her knees financially. The blockade also stopped the import of European fashions.

In the early years of the war, Southern women extended the lives of their fine gowns as long as possible. Often, they restyled them by switching the trimmings and lace from gown to gown, but soon their efforts to maintain a fashion sense seemed futile. By the last years of the war, the gowns were being cut up and remade into uniforms, shirts, underwear, or bandages for the fighting men. Hoops were abandoned and skirts were remade using much less fabric to free the excess yardage for more urgent uses. Since the sewing machine was virtually unknown in the South, all the garments, including shoes, had to be sewn by hand. The industrialized North had sewing machines and could import fabrics so that frequently, after a Southern battle victory, the bodies on the fields were stripped of their clothing, including boots, by victorious soldiers who badly needed to replace garments that were falling apart. It is interesting to note that shortly before the outbreak of war, a Northern inventor had devised a sewing machine heavy enough to sew leather, and for the first time in history boots were made to fit both the left and right foot, so that a soldier did not have to hobble around until his boots stretched to fit his feet. This piece of technology was a great advantage to the Union military and may even have helped to shorten the war.

The garments in this book represent fashions popular during the 1840s and 1850s, a time when stylish wardrobes were still available to the women, men, and children of the South. It should be noted that in several of the pictures, a clothing style from those prewar decades is shown intentionally with a military uniform in use during the Civil War to convey the flavor of the Old South.

Walking Costumes

The woman wears a walking costume of sheer muslin or mull for a summer outing. The soft, belted jacket features shirred bands of fabric that are repeated on the full sleeves. The neckline and cuffs are edged with gathered lace. Her straw bonnet is trimmed with ribbon and silk flowers. The boy wears a short "box" jacket with bell sleeves that are scalloped at the openings. His full-cut trousers are gathered onto a waistband. The girl wears a simple poke bonnet of straw. Her short-sleeved blouse has a tucked front. Her skirt of plaid gingham is worn over pantalets. She wears string-mesh fingerless gloves.

Dressed for a Lesson

A young mother teaches her children to read. She wears a light-colored silk gown with soft collar and cuffs that are scalloped and trimmed with cutwork. Both girls have dresses with long sleeves that balloon at the top. The older girl wears a dropped-shoulder gown that is styled like an adult's dress. The younger child wears a softly pleated skirt and low boots.

A Stylish Family

The parents have bought a toy theater, which their children greet with joy and surprise. At the far left, the grandmother wears a knitted stole over her dark-colored silk gown. Her gathered lace cap has sheer lappets falling to the sides and over the shoulders. The mother wears an evening gown of silk with an overskirt that has three lace tiers topped by ruched ribbon. The shoulder flounce is of the same sheer, edged in lace. The underskirt is of the same fabric as the bodice. The girl by her side wears a dress that has a softly fluted collar and matching ruffle at the yoke; three-quarter-length sleeves, banded at the wrist; and a two-tiered skirt over pantalets that are also banded at the ankle.

The father stands among four of his daughters. He wears a dark suit with a light-colored buttoned vest and tie. The older daughter, who is accompanying her parents to a dinner party, is wearing a long gown of medium-toned silk. Her shoulders are covered, and there is a lace ruffle atop her shoulder flounce. The younger girls wear cotton day dresses, and one wears long pantalets.

Outdoor Wear

The young lady wears a bodice and an overskirt—both of the same silken fabric—that is tucked up so that it flows gracefully to the back. The underskirt is done in a paler color than the bodice. The little girl wears a pastel-colored silk dress with bands of gathered sheer at the neckline and sleeves. Her pantaloons are of white muslin, and she wears white spats.

Gala Wear

The couple is dressed for a gala. The woman's gown is made of light-colored silk. It features a dropped neckline, which is edged with a cuff of embroidered sheer. This sheer is repeated at the base of the skirt in a gathered ruffle that is edged with pearls. The gentleman wears a dark long-tailed frock coat over a light-colored vest and trousers.

Visitors Pay a Call

The seated woman wears a tea gown of watered silk in a medium tone. The gown has a front closure whose buttons are obscured by a silk-embroidered floral motif running from neckline to hem. The collar and modesty are of sheer white lawn. The caller is wearing the winter "undress" uniform typical of the First Regiment of Virginia Volunteers. The uniform is made of gray wool and sports a gold-buckled white bandolier, a gold belt buckle, and gold buttons.

This pair—mother and daughter—have come to call dressed in autumn attire. The mother's walking dress is made of heavy silk; her *manteau,* or cloak, is made of muted plaid wool with silk flounces at the sleeves and hem. The young daughter is dressed in a wool suit in an autumnal color. The shape of the brimless bonnets of the period was known as a "melon" style.

A Thoughtful Pair

The seated woman wears a lightweight silk *robe de chambre,* or dressing gown, edged with a lace panel over her nightdress. Both garments are done in pale tones. Her friend, who has stopped by to pay a call on her way to a concert, wears a brocaded mantle—an open cloak— trimmed with down. Beneath the mantle is a satin gown that is trimmed with sheer pleated flounces worked with *point d'appliqué* in a rose pattern. The rose motif is repeated using silk roses at the opening of the flounces.

Dressed for Dinner

For a quiet dinner at home, this gown of light-colored sheer lawn or gauze, with a shirred bodice that matches the Mameluke-styled sleeves, is an excellent choice. The plunging waist is accented by the voluminous skirt. The gentleman wears a dark hammer-tail jacket with light-colored vest and trousers.

13

A Housedress and a Carriage Dress

The seated woman wears a basic housedress of polished cotton. She is making trim for a future dressmaking project. Her friend wears a carriage dress of light-colored watered silk under a dark velvet wrap. The wrap is trimmed with a broad band of ermine, forming a *pelerine* (short cape) at the neck and encircling the entire garment. The broad hanging sleeves are trimmed in a similar fashion.

Summertime Styles

The woman is dressed in a summer-weight calling gown in a medium-toned watered silk; her white blouse shows at the neck and wrist. Her lace shawl, thrown over a chair, is in a dark color with an overall pattern. The girl wears a light-colored silk dress edged with lace and dominated by a huge, brightly colored and fringed bow of ribbon tied at the waist. She wears stockings and cloth spats with a lace frill edging over the shoes.

15

A Romantic Pair

This romantic couple, caught up in their intimate thoughts, wears casual attire. The young woman is dressed in a simple gown of light-colored cotton. The half-apron worn in front has a brightly colored ribbon band for trim. The young man wears a medium-toned lightweight wool suit with a long frock coat and vest.

A Military Family

A young naval officer is home on leave to see his wife and newborn child. He wears a navy blue uniform with gold trim. Although still in the U.S. Navy, he will soon resign to join the Confederate Navy. His wife is dressed in a light-colored silk negligee enhanced by lace flounces in the front and at the sleeves. Her nightcap is made of lace and ribbon and is worn over a snood of silken net.

The Height of Fashion

The woman's dress, made of taffeta, features a skirt with twenty-four flounces. The long-waisted bodice is accented with a ribbon at the waist. The pagoda-shaped sleeves are edged with taffeta frills, as is the jacket. The chemisette and under-sleeves are made of English point lace. The girl's calling costume is made of a light-colored taffeta edged with scalloped eyelet embroidery and a row of decorative bows down the front. The sleeves have similar eyelet embroidery and bows. The costume is from Madame Demorest's juvenile store in New York.

Bridal Costumes

The bride wears a wedding gown of white silk. The skirt is trimmed with ruches of lace (white lace was often called *blonde* in this era), as are the sleeves and the waist. The veil is made of white net with lace edging. The bride's bonnet, or *casque,* consists of a wreath of white roses and jasmine. The mother of the bride wears a reception dress of silk in a pale tone; it is trimmed with matching ribbon and dyed-to-match lace. The mantle is of black lace, and the coronet cap is made of silk trimmed with matching lace.

Evening Wear

This woman's gown, referred to as *"la demi toilette,"* was suitable for dinner or any evening entertainment. The silk gown has a double skirt; the trim is black velvet edged with black lace and finished with fanciful buttons called *grelots*. The low-set puffed sleeves are in the *jockey* style. Her escort is dressed in the uniform of the Rockbridge Artillery, Army of Northern Virginia, which is gray with a red collar; the cuffs have gold trim and buttons. The uniform is worn with black boots and hat.

A Riding Style

This lady's riding habit of dark blue worsted with self-covered buttons was known as the *"En Cavalier"* style. It has a full-length skirt, a cavalier-influenced scalloped cambric collar, and richly embroidered scalloped cuffs. Her beaver hat is trimmed with colored ribbon and ribbon flowers.

A Military Couple

The woman wears a morning dress of light-colored cotton cambric over a full, gored skirt decorated with fine tucks and embroidery. Panels of puffed cambric edge the gown, revealing the embroidered underskirt. Her chemisette is of finely tucked linen with lace edging; the cap, or *fanchon,* is made of lace with ribbon trim. Her husband is shown getting an early start back to his First Virginia Cavalry Regiment. He is dressed in the uniform of a field officer; it is constructed of medium gray wool and is decorated with gold trim and buttons. His hat, belt, and boots are black.

A Volunteer and Companion

The woman wears an afternoon dress of pale cambric. The three tiers of skirts are accented with eyelet embroidery flounces; they are layered over lace and ribbon underskirts. Medium-toned satin ribbon edges the tiers of the skirt and the collar; the ribbon is used for the decorative bows on the sleeves and skirt. Her escort is uniformed in the officer's "undress" of the First Regiment of Georgia Volunteers, known as the Republican Blues because the uniforms had navy blue *kepis* (caps), jackets, and pale blue pants with a white stripe down the side. Under the officer's black belt is a folded red sash. His buttons and trim are gold.

Out for a Promenade

For her morning promenade at the springs or the seaside, this woman wears pale-toned India muslin, lined in white *glacé* silk. A broad band of the same white silk flanks each side of the skirt. She has a matching mantilla of the same fabric; it features three *volants* (flounces or tiers) edged with lace. Her broad straw hat is called a "Leghorn Pamela" and is decorated with white veiling, lace, ribbon, and silk flowers. Her companion, a trooper from the First Virginia Cavalry Regiment, wears a gray uniform with a black collar, cuffs, and black braid trim. His hat, belt, and boots are black. He has a gold braid hatband, buttons, and buckles.

Spring Walking Fashions

A mother and her daughter wear spring walking dresses. The daughter's dress is made of light-toned *challie* (a lightweight fabric combining wool and silk). Her *basque,* or jacket, is long and full, giving the appearance of a double skirt. The outfit is profusely decorated with buttons. Her Leghorn straw hat has a fall of black lace and ostrich plumes. Her mother wears a light-colored, lightweight silk dress. The skirt's triple flounces are ornamented with side panels that are decorated with darker ribbon latticework, as are the upper sleeves. The bodice and skirt edges are also finished in ribbon. Her straw bonnet is trimmed with lace, ribbon, and silk almond blossoms.

Dressed for Dinner

The woman's lightweight dinner dress is made of grenadine with pale polka dots; it is trimmed with ribbon ruches the same color as the dots. The dress has a double skirt; the sleeves have triple flounces. The bodice, or corsage, is cut low for evening, but is worn here with a fill, or *berthé,* whose collar fits to the throat. The lace cap is trimmed with satin ribbon matching the ruches. She is accompanied by a cavalryman of the Hampton Legion of South Carolina Volunteers. His blue-gray jacket has a gold collar, cuffs, and trim. His trousers are a darker blue-gray. He wears a plumed felt hat and leather tie, belt, and holsters.

Dressed for a Formal Reception

The woman wears an opera cloak to a "hop" and full-dress reception. Her silk gown is covered with white flounces. The cloak (or *sortie*), in the style of the hooded burnous, is made of boldly colored silk and edged with heavy, intricately designed silk fringe. The hood is weighted with silk. Her escort is an Old Dominion rifle-man of the Sixth Battalion of Virginia Volunteers. His uniform of gray wool is worn with a white *baldric* (or bandolier) with a gold buckle. The buttons, belt buckle, and insignia on his hat are also gold. He wears a black hatband, bill, belt, and boots; his trim, chevrons, and hat pompon are bright green.

A Pair of Cotillion Dresses

These two women wear evening dresses suitable for a cotillion or formal reception. The gown on the left, of brightly colored silk, has a skirt with three crepe flounces formed by narrow *quillings* (rows of gathers). The same trimming appears on the berthé of the corsage, which also has *cordons* (ropes) of silk leaves like those on the skirt. Silk camellias are worn at the bosom. At the right is a dress of pastel-colored watered silk, with a flounced skirt edged with bands of satin ribbon. Fichu-shaped *bretelles* (shoulder straps or suspenders) are edged in ribbon to cover the shoulders and cross in front at the waist. The chemisette and sleeves are also trimmed with ribbon.

Mother and Daughter Walking Costumes

The girl's dress is made of plaid *Valentia* (a faille of wool and cotton). Her cloak of woolen *rep* (a corded fabric) has richly colored stripes. The mother's walking dress is made of dark, heavy silk with a front panel finished in a checked pattern of black velvet and trimmed with double rows of velvet buttons. The cloak, called a "Cherbourg," has a dark ground with colored stripes and is cut on the bias; it has an over-cape that is round behind but ends in heavily tasseled points. The entire cloak is edged with heavy silk galloon that picks up one of the colors in the stripes.

A Popular Prewar Style

The *tablier* style of day dress was particularly popular with prewar Southern ladies. "Tablier" means apron, and the trim is arranged so as to indicate a complete apron in the front of the skirt. The gown is made of two shades of silk bands and has folded and crossed bretelles at the shoulder. Fringe defines the bands of the skirt, and self-covered buttons enhance the lines. A fringed umbrella and a cartwheel Leghorn straw hat complete the ensemble. This sergeant of the Fourth Battalion of Virginia Volunteers wears a navy blue uniform with medium blue trim, chevrons, and hat pompon. He wears a folded red sash around his waist.

Dressed for a Sunday Outing

The woman wears a manteau of moiré knit, lace, and chenille braid. When spread out, the garment makes three-quarters of a circle. Her pale-colored silk gown has black pin stripes. Her lace cap has a large bow of ribbon at the throat. Her daughter wears a silk dress trimmed with narrow gathered ribbon. The chemisette and sleeves are of sheer muslin. Her muslin pantalets are trimmed with lace. Her son wears a richly colored velvet blouse. His trousers are edged with a flounce and a narrow border of lace. His stockings are a light-colored plaid.

Officers and a Lady

Flanked by two officers of the First Regiment of Virginia Volunteers, the woman wears a dinner dress of brightly colored glacé silk with a short fringe-edged upper skirt under a pointed waistline. The lower skirt is trimmed with velvet bands and silk fringe, as are the corsage and sleeves. Her gathered lace collar has bands of velvet ribbon. The colonel [left] wears a navy blue uniform with gold buttons and trim. His plumed hat has gold insignia. The captain [right], in the Montgomery Guard, Company C, wears a green claw-tailed jacket and hat, both trimmed with gold. The cockade on his hat has two upper tiers of white feathers and a lower one of green. His trousers are blue-gray. Both men wear a red sash under their belts.